WHISPERS OF A PRISM HEART

WHISPERS
OF A
PRISM HEART

BY VERNAJH PINDER

Whispers of A Prism Heart

Printed in the United States of America

First Printing, April 2025

ISBN 979-8-89379-507-3

THANK YOU FOR PURCHASING THIS BOOK

check out the official playlist

scan here

@vernthepoet

ALSO BY VERNAJH PINDER,

Hope You Don't Get Famous
Deviant: Chronicles of Pride (Anthology)
Sometime Superheroes Need Saving Too

Table of Contents

ACKNOWLEDGEMENT

To my grandfather, Emery Symonette, thank you for everything. I am who I am because you inspired me to be.

To my parents, thank you for all the sacrifices you made. The older I get, the more I understand. Thank you for constantly pushing me to be the best version of myself. Thank you for always believing in me and supporting my dreams. I fly because you taught me how to.

To my siblings, thank you for showing up for me in more ways than one.

To my friends who have been with me every step of the way, thank you for going on this journey and always listening to my poetry and crazy ideas. Thank you for making me feel less crazy than I think I am; I love you guys to the moon and back.

To all the boys and girls out there still hiding in fear, I hope the world will be a safe space one day, and you can be who you are without care or harm.

Vernajh Pinder

To RG, thank you for letting me know that love
was out there waiting for me, and I just had to
open my eyes up to find it. Thank you for
reminding me that it's okay to love and allow
yourself to be loved. But, also, in order for love
to come, you have to be willing to stand (or sit) in
your truth. You taught me that love was real.

"Owning our story and loving ourselves through that process is the bravest thing we'll ever do." – Brené Brown,

CHAPTER 1

IDENTITY

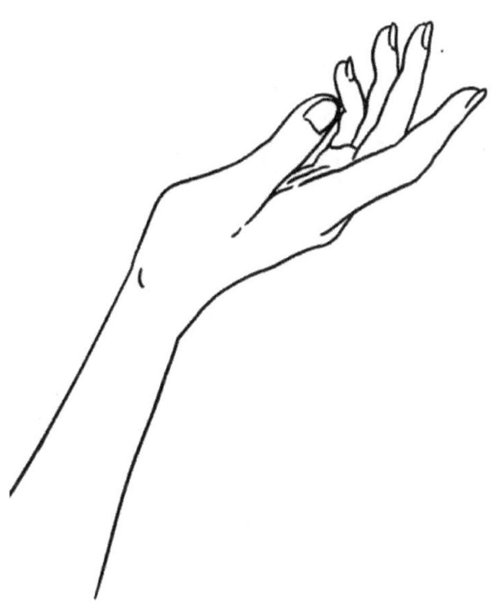

The Burden of Truth - A Short Story

I pace back and forth in the diner. "This is it," I think to myself. I'm about to tell my best friend that I'm gay. I take a deep breath and try to steady myself. I hear the engine of your car before I see you. My heart quickens, and panic sets in.

"Amari, are you okay?" Sheila's voice pulls me back to reality, and I feel her hand on my shoulder. "How about we sit down?" she suggests. "What's got you so flustered?"

Eyes fixed forward, I whisper, "I'm doing it, Sheila. I'm going to tell him."

The color drains from her face. "Are you sure about this?" she asks.

I shake my head no. She squeezes my hand and presses a kiss to my forehead. Just then, the bell jingles above the door, and I watch as Blake walks in. I've known him all my life. We grew up in the same neighborhoods, went to the same schools, played the same sports. We've been inseparable, and I'm hoping that after today, we continue to be.

"What's up, A? What's so urgent that we couldn't talk about it over the phone and had to meet in person?"

I'm petrified, barely able to muster a "hi." A look of worry crosses Blake's face, and I finally find the strength to say, "I need to tell you something."

"What is it? Come on, out with it."

"I-I-I," I stutter. "I'm—"

"Spit it out, A. You're starting to scare me."

I inhale deeply and exhale the truth. "I'm gay."

The words taste rancid coming off my tongue. I look over at Blake, who suddenly bursts into laughter. "Whew, good one," he chuckles. "Seriously, what did you want to tell me?"

I stare at him, my face expressionless, and then I see it—the moment realization dawns. The wrinkles on his forehead deepen, his face darkens with something heavier than frustration. Anger. His pupils dilate, his eyes becoming vacant, soulless. And then the hate bubbles over as he begins to spew venomous words.

It's like I'm trapped in my own mind, watching helplessly as he transforms before me. Blake reaches for me, but I instinctively leap back, stepping out of the booth. The diner falls silent. All eyes are on us. Sheila rushes over.

"Alright, boys, maybe we should take a minute," she suggests, her voice cautious.

Blake glares at me, rage radiating off him in waves. "You're dead to me, A," he seethes. "You're so fucking dead to me."

Then he storms out, slamming the door behind him. I watch as he hops into his car and peels out of the parking lot. My heart pounds. He speeds down the road, taking a sharp right—and then it happens.

A car slams into his. The impact sends his car spinning, tires

screeching. It skids for at least a hundred yards before coming to a stop.

"Someone call 911!" I scream, already running toward the wreck.

Sheila is two steps behind me, but my feet are on autopilot. "Blake! No, Blake!" I mumble under my breath. And then—

His car explodes.

I keep running, but Sheila grabs my arm, yanking me back. I don't know when the tears start, but suddenly I'm sobbing, uncontrollably. Sheila wraps her arms around me, holding me up as my knees threaten to give out.

This is my fault.

I'm the reason he's dead.

My best friend is dead because of me.

I jolt upright in bed, drenched in sweat, heart pounding. My breath is ragged as I scan the dark room. Across from me, Blake stirs, his groggy voice cutting through the silence.

"You okay, A?"

I whisper, "Yeah," and lay back down, my mind spinning.

Do I still want to go through with this?

Whispers of A Prism Heart

I am little echoes,
Fragments of every sound I've heard,
Little microcosms of each reality
That I've dared to live.

I am tiny molecules
Of those young and old,
Those who walked this plane before me
And those still waiting to arrive.

I am the portrait
Of dreams painted by my ancestors,
The love that dwells within—
A river flowing exceedingly and abundantly.

I am these little pieces
Of everyone I've ever met.
I am the touch of those who have loved me,
In this life or the next,

I am who they said I could never be—
Young, happy, free.
I am the winds that dance with the leaves,
The fire that refuses to die.

I am who they said I could never be—
The untold stories, finally free
That's who I am.
That's who I'll always be.

Vernajh Pinder

I've been defined by labels
All my life.
Their words sharp and unrelenting,
Have carved me into pieces
I never chose for myself.

I've been told who to be,
Confined to the narrow limits
Of their expectations,
Where stepping outside was unforgiving.

Labels have clouded
My entire existence.
And the more they have pushed them onto me,
The more the weight of their words sank into my
skin.

When they say it enough—
That you are small,
That you are broken,
That you are nothing—
You start to believe it.
You start to carry their judgments
As if they were truths
Born into your very being.

For years, I carried those lies.
I believed them when they said
I was black, queer, and nothing—
A defect outside the lines,
Unworthy of respect,

Whispers of A Prism Heart

Unworthy of love,
Trapped in the margins
Of being too much and not enough.

But no more.
I have peeled their labels from my skin;
Their words are not my truth.
I am not a silhouette
Cut from the fabric of their fear.

I am who I am—
Unapologetic, unyielding.
I am art they cannot silence.
It is not my responsibility
To fit into the boxes they've built
To contain me.

I write my own story,
One word, one breath, one moment at a time.
And it is mine, and mine alone—
Untouched by their small imaginations,
Unbound by their fleeting judgments.

Do you kiss your mother with those lips,
Where lies hide on the surface
And force their way into lives,
Only to leave wreckage in their wake?

Do you smile at your father,
With those eyes that keep secrets?
Whose true nature is never present,
Because you've learned to let your eyes tell lies.

Do you hug your sister
With those hands that spread hate?
And when clenched,
Leave bruises and hurt in their wake?

Do you listen to your brother,
Or do your ears occlude,
Like when the scream of your lovers
Is choked out of their mouths?

Does your heart have an inkling of love?
Does it live without conditions,
Or does its unscrupulous nature
Destroy those who try to hold it?

Is your soul as dark as a black hole?
Or is there some semblance of love inside?
Because you are the master of faces,
The original Jekyll and Hyde.

The drum beats within,
A war that I cannot win.
Love as you may,
But never love who you are,
For the hopeless heart
Will lead you astray.

Vernajh Pinder

There is remarkable beauty
In rejecting the trajectory
Society sets for your destiny.

There is earnest freedom
In living life as you choose,
Not as they would have you do.

There is endless power
In straying from the norm,
For we are all born
To carve our own freedom.

Whispers of A Prism Heart

Who I am now
Is a mere drop
Of who I have the potential to be.

Yet the journey ahead feels lonely,
A beauty just out of my reach.

Each step I take whispers back,
"You are closer than you think,"
But the echoes of an imposter
Remind me how far I've yet to go.

Still, even within dubiety,
There is the hope of becoming—
A spark that holds the flame
Of all I can be.

Who I am now
Feels minuscule,
But there is always the potential
Of who I can be.

My brain has felt hazy these past few months. It's as if I'm losing touch with reality—or at least losing my touch. Before, I considered myself one of the greats, someone who could weave words together like the strings on a tennis racket. But now, my thoughts are scattered, tumbling in every direction, and I can't seem to catch even one, no matter how directly it comes toward me. Instead, I let them pass because it takes too much energy to fight back.

I used to be able to sit for hours, crafting poems that reached deep into the soul, poems that sang soliloquies before the curtains fell. Who am I without writing? What do I become when the thing I love most in this world no longer seems to love me back?

Vernajh Pinder

He was a prisoner,
Trapped behind the corners of his mind,
His own worst enemy, it seems, time after time.
And though he tried to escape,
His resistance was futile.

So he found a corner with his name on it,
And decided to sit for a while.

The screams got louder,
It was more than he could take.
The echoes of those before us,
His mind ready to break.

He could hear the names they called him,
The labels stuck inside.
You could see the pain it cost him,
Stuck between his eyes.

But no more, he thought,
Not anymore.
He refused to play this game,
He would get through that door.
So, he got up, walked to the door, and shook it
open.

I've spent most of my life trying to appease others,
Trying to fit the molds they've set forth,
Being the puppet whose strings they pull,
Dancing in every direction they lead me.
And I still can't figure out who I am.
But I don't want to let anyone down.
And I wonder if it's the people-pleaser in me,
Who's afraid to cut the strings that pull me in every direction.

Vernajh Pinder

Some people were born
Knowing who they are.
Others, like myself,
Had to fight tooth and nail
To figure it out,
Because being who we are
Wasn't okay at all.

So we had two choices:
Figure out who
We wanted to be,
Or be who they
Told us we should be.

No more can I sit Idle
and take a passenger seat
in my own life.

I am the driver
I control my own destiny.

Journal Entry 4 - 1/28/24

Today, I've been struggling with these thoughts of black despondency. They aren't as bad as they were a few days ago, but enough to make me question my existence. It's funny though, because I know I deserve to be here, but sometimes it feels otherwise. Like, I know I'm loved, but most times I question it.

It's like God put all this talent inside of me, but am I using it? Am I using my abilities to their fullest potential? Am I just the mistakes I've made? Do I not deserve grace? Yet, why do I not give myself any? Why can I show that grace to everyone else but not to myself? I am worthy of love.

Sometimes, I get a little jealous seeing my friends happy and in relationships. They deserve love and happiness, but don't I deserve it too? Why do they get to have it and I don't? Although, I also don't know what they had to go through to get it, and I get that, but sometimes it really makes me question myself and my worthiness.

It's funny though, all my life I wanted to come out, and I did (sort of). I came out to a select few people, but I still feel like I'm hiding myself. I'm still afraid of what others would say, how they would view me. I shouldn't. I shouldn't care about what people think of me, but the reality is, my reality is that I do.

I look at my reflection,
A wave of nausea crashes over me.

I hate that I'm this way—
Broken,
An unfixable pawn in a game I didn't choose.
I hate this feeling.

I hate the fact that
I've been taught to hate myself,
To think less of who I am
Because they say something's wrong with me.

I'm not supposed to be wired this way.
I have mental health issues.

Maybe conversion therapy will help—
But I just feel lost.

I feel like my world is coming down,
Crashing fast,
Or maybe I set it on fire
Because I can't breathe.

I'm slowly fading,
And there's no light at the end.

So, do I live in my truth?
Or continue to hide?

To grow into the person you're meant to be,
You must first get tired of who you are now.
Until you feel uncomfortable with where you are,
And who you are, nothing will change.

Whispers of A Prism Heart

Remnants of me wander through the dark,
Floating, like liquid void of shape.

I hear the silence through the trees,
And the wind blows.

Where do I go?
What's left for me?

How do I run,
When my feet won't carry me?

They have a mind of their own,
And my hands, they tremble.

I am just a lost boy,
With no place to call home.

Find me.
Free me.

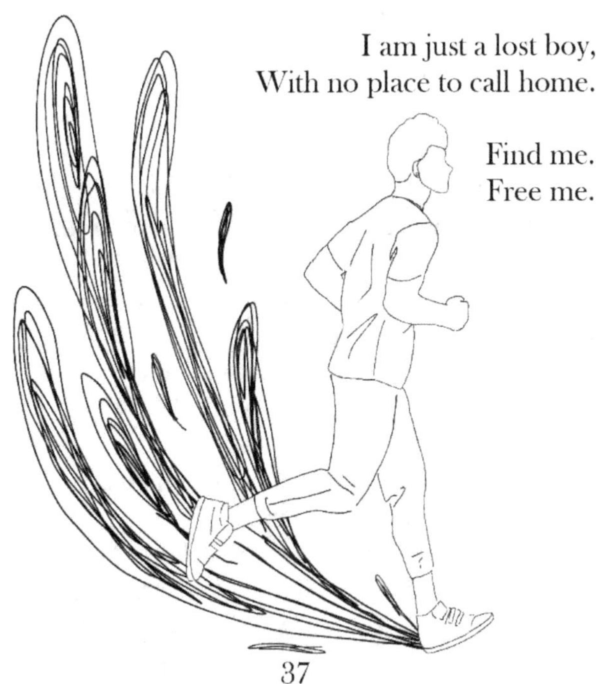

Vernajh Pinder

I have always been afraid.
I revert to being child-like, cowering and
trembling.
"Don't be too much, and for God's sake, don't
you dare do too much."
Because who are you?
Who do you think you are to breathe the same
air as us?
To be in the same spaces as us, as our kids?
Exist just enough, but don't you dare take up too
much space.

I've lived my life where the rules of my existence
Were dictated by those around me.
Each day, I became a shell of my former self,
And I watched— a prisoner in my own story—
As the life that once existed inside me dissipated.

I lose track sometimes.
Fatigue dances across my eyelids, and I go with it.
It's funny how easy it is to get caught up in the
noise.
How you lose yourself with every moment you
don't allow yourself to be free.
Or how the more you allow yourself to be lost,
The more you'll never be found.

You build this mirage of small moments,
Trying to hold onto happiness—
To hold onto this version of freedom,
Carved by the remnants of broken dreams.

38

Whispers of A Prism Heart

Until it's too late, and now you hesitate,
To reflect on the person you've become—
A vacant soul, dead on the inside.

I'm 16 again.
I've just graduated high school, and it's a late
night in early September.
I'm sitting in the dark, watching coming-out
videos.
That's when I stumble upon Troye Sivan and his
coming-out story.
I watch his video over and over, praying to
whatever god might be listening,
Hoping that one day, it'd be me.
That one day, I'd no longer be shackled by
embarrassment.

I listen to Blue Neighbourhood for the first time,
And sadness consumes me.
I've been conditioned to believe that love will
never find me.
I'm queer—an anathema to the world—or at least,
that's how I've been made to feel.
But still, I long. I hope. I dream.
I want, more than anything, to escape that place.

I tell myself that nothing will change if I stay.
But if I leave, maybe—just maybe—I can be free.
If I pack my bags and go, I can create a new life,
One where I'm not bound by shame.
There's an undertone to that hope, though—
One I didn't fully understand back then.

But that didn't happen.
I lost myself instead.

Vernajh Pinder

I've long carried
The dreams and desires
Of those I've encountered
Along my journey.

Their hopes and dreams
For me echo,
And sometimes, I confuse them
As my own.

Whispers of A Prism Heart

I miss the person you used to be,
So full of life and hope.
But your optimism has left you,
Like an ocean receding from the shore.
Your innocence, a mirage,
Lingering behind,
Tied to the false hope you once believed.
That hope was lost a long time ago.

Now, what's left is a reality
You refuse to live in.
So, you let life walk on by,
Paralyzed by fear.
You do not live.
You no longer dream of a future,
Because you are trapped,
And you allow yourself to remain trapped.
Unwilling to fight,
Because you lost your will to fight
Several eons ago.

Oh, how I miss him—
So full of life and hope,
He who dared to live
And refused to let his circumstances
Define who he could become.
He who would rather die living
Than live only to die.
He who lived and ruled with kindness,
Refusing to let the hardness of the world

Suck the innocence out of him.
Unafraid, unapologetic,
Unwilling to compromise
For things that would steal his peace.
An inspiration to many,
And one who was always inspired.
Oh, how I miss him.

I've stayed silent on issues
I shouldn't have.
Laughed too hard at jokes
That made me uncomfortable.
Strived so hard to fit in,
To be who people want me to be,
Fit within this perfect picture I created—
That I've lost track of who I really am.

The boy I was trying to find,
His picture on milk cartons,
Lining shelves everywhere.
Have you seen him?
Have you seen the boy I once was?
The boy who dreamed of changing the world,
The boy who believed in love and happily ever
afters,
The boy who wanted more out of his life.

Where'd he go? Have you seen him?
Because for the longest time, he's been missing.

Vernajh Pinder

I was told as a child that I was going to hell.
That because I didn't subscribe to
heteronormative beliefs,
I was going to burn in an eternal fire.
I cried.
Day after day, I would drop to my bloodied
knees
And ask God to change me.
I would beg him to take these feelings away
Because I didn't want to burn.

I had felt the heat from the grill,
And knew that I didn't want to be charred.
Then I would be okay for a few days,
But like clockwork, these feelings would come
back
Because that was just who I was.

Religion made me believe I was an
abomination—
That I didn't deserve to be here.
That my life was minuscule,
And if I didn't change,
If I didn't subscribe to what they said,
I was damned to hell.
For a long time, I believed that.
But I also believe that God is love.

If God made us in His likeness and image,
Am I not a piece of Him?

Does He not love all His children, despite their
flaws?
Did Jesus not command us to love our neighbors
as ourselves,
Yet we condemn and judge them?

There are moments when we feel so lost,
Like our purpose for living has dissipated into
nothingness.
We feel like tiny atoms floating in space,
Meagerly existing in limbo.

In those moments, when you feel lost,
Take time to reconnect with yourself.

My demons hide,
Deeply embedded in my subconscious,
Lying in wait,
For the perfect opportunity.

Vernajh Pinder

I have hidden myself for so long,
Afraid that embracing my truth would reduce me
To a meaningless speck of dust.
That my queerness would offend those around
me,
And somehow make them smaller.

I dimmed my light,
Allowing others to shine through me.
I have celebrated everyone,
And in doing so,
I have forgotten to celebrate myself.

I never wanted this. There, I said it. I never
wanted to be the most hated human being on the
planet, but here I am. Then to add to that, queer
and black—a death sentence. Coupled with years
of internalized homophobia, and you have me.
I never wanted this life for myself, but somehow,
here I am. I feel like I've let my family, my
friends, my country down. I feel like I've let the
world down.

Every day, I'm fighting with the feeling of
whether I'll fly or watch myself fall. I'm not in
distress, but most days, I want to climb to the top
of the highest building, Close my eyes, and free-
fall. But that sounds too painful. So, sometimes,
I try to cut my wrist because that feels easier,
And I watch as the blood glides down my hand
and drips off my elbow. Drip. Drop. Drip. Drop.
Such a soothing sound, and the pain—it feels so
comforting.

But that didn't work. When I woke up, I realized
what I had done, and I cried. I did the same after
I slit my arms. I cried. I cried because I wanted
to be here, But the pressure of living up to
everyone's standards, To their idea of who I
should be, really fucking sucked.

So, most days, I trap myself in a closet. And it's
funny because I'm not in the closet, But I'm a
closeted gay man. I spend most of my life living

in the shadows of my former self, Because I
don't want to offend anybody.

Therefore, I shrink and shrink until I'm just as
minuscule as I've been made to feel all my life—
until I'm the smallest element known to man.
The implications of being a queer black man?
They suck.

I see so many people living their lives so freely,
so happily, And then I see myself. I see traces of
my true self, but I discard them so fast, That any
glint of hope I dream of is gone before I blink
again. Then, a wave of jealousy hits me, and I
envy them. I envy how free they are, but I don't
hate them. I hate how they don't care about what
others think, And I wish they could be me.
I long for the day when I could just be... free.
Where I don't have to care about what others
think of me, And I can live life. Where I can
embrace who I am, as I truly am. But that dream
seems too far-fetched to ever be my reality. It
seems to be an illusion that continues to taunt
me, knowing it will never be.

I remember hearing Same Love on the radio for
the first time, driving down the street, headed
home with my grandfather, And I thought to
myself, "Maybe one day." I always dreamed of go

I realize that I hold onto a lot of things because I need to feel needed. I find my worth in how other people value my strengths, my capabilities, and who I am as a person. I never felt important as a kid, so I spent most of my time alone, even though I didn't want to be. It was also safer inside because we live in a cruel world.

One day, I hope I can stop seeking validation and approval from others and instead look within myself for it. I hope I can find peace and happiness within me, because that's where it counts the most.

I no longer wish to call back the older, previous
versions of myself.
Each time I pick up the phone, I hinder myself
from planting roots and growing.
I starve myself of water, sun, and food—
The very things I need not only to thrive but to
survive.

I no longer write love letters to my future self,
Hoping and praying that I made it, that life gets
better,
That I'll be happy.
By doing this, I starve myself of present-day
happiness—
Of living in the moment and showing up for
myself in the here and now.

I put to rest these obsessions with past and future
versions of me,
Ones that either no longer serve me or that I
haven't met.
I am creating a space to exist in the now,
To love myself in the now.
The past is just that—the past.
The future is not yet here.
Therefore, I owe it to myself (and to the past and
future versions of me)
To live in the here and now.

Whispers of A Prism Heart

26 years in the making,
And out of everything I've done,
This still feels like the hardest thing.

Those words make existing feel like
It's the hardest thing to do,
And I can still hear them.

The music replays in my ears,
Over and over,
And just like that broken little boy,
I hide.

But then, I lift the needle and flip the record—
It's time to play a different song.

Vernajh Pinder

I remember hearing Same Love on the radio for
the first time, driving down the street, headed
home with my grandfather, and I thought to
myself, "Maybe one day." I always dreamed of
going off to school, so I worked my ass off to go,
Butuse I thought if I came to America, I'd be
able to be free. But, I think I trapped myself
deeper into a closet.

Homophobia is so ingrained in me that no
matter how far I run from it, No matter how
much I walk out of a closet, I still feel like I'm
trapped. It's dark and cold in here, and most
days, I feel so alone. The irony of being
surrounded by so many people but always feeling
so alone. It's a feeling I just can't seem to shake.
Loneliness. It's like everywhere I go, every
country I start over in, Every friend I make, I still
feel lonely. Maybe that's who I'm meant to be—a
lonely wayfaring stranger With no place to call
home. And it sucks that my actual home feels
like a death sentence, Because everyone there
thinks queer people are abominations.

Growing up, I heard some of the most hurtful
and hateful things from family members,
From people I thought were friends, from those
who promised to protect the innocent.
Ain't it funny, though, to think I'd willingly
choose to be the most hated human being on the
planet—twice? It's a death sentence I'd never

wish on anyone. Maybe I'm not supposed to fall in love. Maybe I'm not supposed to ever escape the loneliness that follows, Like a shadow over my head. Maybe I'm not supposed to be here.

I'm grateful for the friends that love me and allow me to be myself. I don't know where I'd be without them. The safe spaces they've created for me. The friends who go out of their way to make sure I have the opportunities to be myself. If it weren't for them, I may not be here today. So, to them, I owe myself— All my love and my happiness, Because I'd have none without them.

Vernajh Pinder

Every day, I lose a part of who I am
In the midst of becoming.
I must shed my skin—
And allow myself to be rebirthed
Into the person I was destined to be.

I knew I was queer when I was four years old.
Even as a young child, I was certain of who I was.
My interests always differed from those of the
boys in the neighborhood. I loved playing
outside—running barefoot in the streets, playing
tag, football, and even basketball (though,
truthfully, I've always hated basketball). But I
also enjoyed doing things society considered
feminine as well like sewing, cooking, poetry, and
creating.

That certainty stayed with me until society, and
even my own family, taught me otherwise. They
told me it was just a phase, something that would
pass. Did they know any better? Perhaps not.
Perhaps they didn't understand the damage they
caused, forcing a child to hide who they truly
were—to stuff their identity into a metaphorical
closet, no pun intended.

As I grew up, I heard some of the harshest words
from places that should have been sanctuaries of
love. The people who were supposed to protect
and uplift me became the ones whose words cut
the deepest. Maybe they thought they were
protecting me—from a society, a country,
unwilling to accept me. But their protection felt
like rejection. I began to hate myself so much
that I tried to pray it away. When prayer failed, I
turned to something darker.

Overwhelmed by the combination of family conflicts and a world that felt like it had no place for me, I decided I didn't want to be here anymore. I wrote a letter and swallowed two bottles of pills.

It didn't work. Perhaps diet pills weren't meant to end a life, or maybe it just wasn't my time. Maybe—just maybe—my story wasn't finished.

Since then, I've struggled with my identity. I've often felt like I was only half-living, unable to fully embrace who I am. It's exhausting to live in a way that makes you feel like being yourself is somehow "too much." But that was then. Now, I'm on a path of healing. I've learned to allow myself to simply be.
Therapy has been a cornerstone of my journey. I drink a lot of water, and I focus on nurturing my inner child—that little boy who still carries so much pain. Healing takes time, but it's worth every moment. With each step, I reclaim parts of myself I thought were lost forever.

A significant part of my growth has been learning about forgiveness. I write this now with the understanding that I have a great relationship with my family. Yet healing also requires honesty. Loving someone doesn't mean ignoring the ways they've hurt you. It's about finding the courage to acknowledge it and still choosing love.

As I reflect, I hope society continues to evolve—
to become more accepting of people who are
different. No child should grow up in an
environment where hate takes root. Disagreeing
with someone's identity or lifestyle doesn't have
to lead to disrespect or hate. We can coexist with
differing perspectives, respecting one another's
humanity.

Groupthink is a dangerous phenomenon. It
often pushes people to fear and reject what they
don't understand. This fear perpetuates cycles of
misunderstanding and hate, leading to division.
As Erykah Badu said, "They who play it safe are
quick to assassinate what they do not understand.
They move in packs, ingesting more and more
fear with every act of hate on one another. They
feel most comfortable in groups, less guilt to
swallow. They are us. This is what we have
become. Afraid to respect the individual. A
single person within a circumstance can move
one to change. To love herself, to evolve."

I've chosen to evolve. To respect myself. To
forgive and love. And I hope the world continues
to grow in love too. Because every individual
deserves a chance to simply be.

Vernajh Pinder

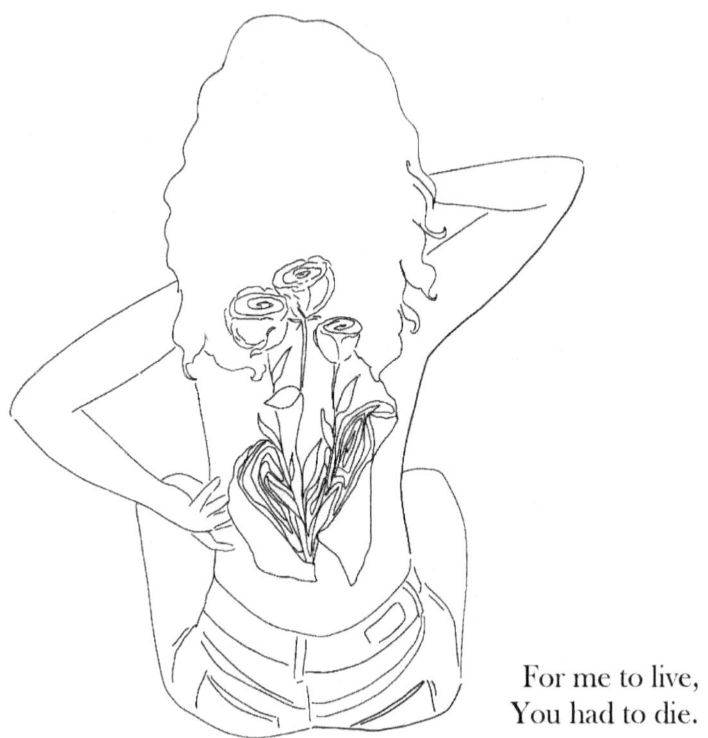

For me to live,
You had to die.

Your absence became my mirror,
Reflecting truths I never dared to face.

I had to lose you,
Surrender the familiar,
To uncover the roots of who I am.

In the silence you left behind,
I found the voice to become.

"Love does not begin and end the way we seem to think it does. Love is a battle; love is a war; love is a growing up." - James Baldwin

CHAPTER 2

Whether I live my truth or not, people are still going to talk—and that's their prerogative. They don't deserve to have that kind of control over me. It's okay for me to simply be me. There are people who will love me for who I am, no matter who I am or who I love.

Who you love doesn't make you any less lovable than anyone else. It doesn't mean you don't deserve love, because you do. You are worthy of love. Unconditional love. The kind of love that comes and sits with you, quietly, when you need it. The love that makes you smile for no reason. A love that kisses your forehead and tells you you're beautiful. The kind of love that makes you feel safe, secure, and seen.

A love that lasts across galaxies, through lifetimes, and across universes. The love that pulls you back to the present when you've lost your way. You deserve that kind of love—and if you keep going, if you keep surviving, it'll find you.

I love you. I know life feels strange right now, but it'll be okay. You'll be okay. Life will be okay. Everything will be alright.

At first, it came like a whisper—silent and gentle.
I couldn't hear it, but I felt it, and knew it was
there.

Next, it came as a punch to the gut.
It was too hard to ignore.

The butterflies would cartwheel in my stomach
every time I saw you.

It wasn't easy to ignore anymore; I was falling for
you.

I didn't understand it at first, so I tried to get as
far away from you as possible.

But you wouldn't let me.
You weren't willing to let our friendship go.

Not yet, at least.

Whispers of A Prism Heart

You make me feel
As if I am the only one
Existing in this world you've created for us,
Where time stands still, and even the sun holds
her breath.
And I can't help it—
I'm falling for you.

But I throw caution
To the wind,
For I've traveled this road before,
A road that was once filled with hope,
Only to end in shards of my heart
Scattered across oblivion.

I'm afraid—
Afraid that if I love you
Like I've loved past lovers,
I'll be left again with nothing but
The haunting whispers of promises unkept,
And turmoil as my sole and eager companion.

Because they've always left.
And it was me who remained,
Picking up the pieces of myself
From the wreckage they left behind.

So, I stand here now,
At the edge of this cliff,
Unsure if I can give you
All of me, all my love—

Vernajh Pinder

For the roads I've walked
Are paved with heartbreak I cannot unfeel.

Yet, there is magic in the way
You look at me,
As if you see not just my scars,
But the galaxies I hide within them.
And maybe—just maybe—
This road will lead somewhere new.

"You know you'll get hurt, yet you still put yourself through the heartache," the soul whispered to the heart.

"Why do you allow yourself permission to be hurt over and over?"

Frustrated, the heart replied, "I've always wanted love. A love that is wild and free, that goes beyond logic and reason. A love that embraces the thrill and passion shines through. A love as pure as fire- one that cannot be extinguished."

The soul paused for a moment before responding. With calmness, it said, "Sometimes we have to look beneath the surface and peek into depths unknown. You must sit with yourself in silence and be still. Find out what you truly want because love is not a fleeting emotion, but a choice of the soul."

It continued, "Sometimes patience is key. Do not haste, but let life's flow help you to discover the rhythm of love. Let the alchemy of your rhythm be your guide, and do not be distracted by the guise of illusion."

The heart smiled, for it knew that the soul was right.

Vernajh Pinder

We sway in the breeze,
Hand in hand.

Basking in the luminance of the moon,
Chest to chest.

Left to right, right to left,
Cheek to cheek.

We let our souls dance,
Hearts open.

Sand beneath our feet,
Lip to lip.

While the ocean sings to us,
Ears asleep.

Not the whispers nor sounds of country
Could tear apart
The love we had radiating
On that ethereal eve.

My heart will never forget,
The way your smile
Made my insides sing.
The way your touch
Made me glow like Venus,
All these devout memories
That still linger.

I've held on to this idea of us for quite some
time,
Hoping that you'd grow tired of your past lovers
And find your way back to the home I built for
us—
A home I bled for.
Brick by brick, piece by piece, I tried to make it
perfect.
Not just any home, but our perfect home.

I thought this time would be different.
I thought that when I wove this home together
with every shred of love I had left,
You'd come.
I thought this time, you would come.
But my love, I've come to realize,
Is not a magnet strong enough to pull someone
who isn't willing to be drawn.

Perhaps you don't love me the way I thought you
still did—
Or even the way I still love you.
And that truth cuts deeper than a knife.
It hurts that I must accept that the memories we
created
Must now be left behind, abandoned—
Like old photographs in a home that's on fire.
It pains me even more to admit that the dreams I
long dreamed for us,
The potential for a future, will never come to
fruition.

And yet, staying here, clinging to the only
semblance of happiness I ever felt,
Feels like a quiet death.
The love I poured into this home is suffocating
me now.
I've come to understand that letting you go isn't
about giving up;
It's about setting my heart free.

So, though it aches, I must will myself to walk
away.
I must leave this home, this dream, and all the
love I still have for you.
Because holding on to you is slowly killing me.

Vernajh Pinder

We met in the silence,
When the world forgot to rush.
Moments of rapidness—
Too fragile to last.

Though those moments were enough
To bind me
In this feeling,
I didn't know
I'd been seeking.

Your eyes were a doorway,
A warm invitation
To nowhere
And everywhere—
All at the same time.

And for a millisecond,
I let myself dream
We could exist
In more than this moment.

But transient things
Are that for a reason—
Too beautiful to linger,
Too perfect to stay.

You left before my mouth
Could say what my heart
Wanted it to,
Before reality

Could ask us questions
We weren't ready to answer.
We would never be
Ready to answer.

Now, I carry the ghost of you,
A haunting reminder
That sometimes love
Isn't meant to be kept in a jar—
Just felt.

It's funny how the people you meet can change
so much of who you are—
How their little habits become part of you.
You become so connected that being separated
from them can hurt.

Whispers of A Prism Heart

I've always pondered the idea of love.
I've often wondered: is it a fleeting feeling?
A feeling that comes and goes,
Like shifts in the wind or breaths we take
Until our last one.
For so long, I thought of love as temporary,
As fragile as our fleeting existence on this planet.

But lately, I've begun to question:
Does love transcend death?
Is it an eternal force that lingers beyond space
and time?
Can it tether souls across infinite distances and
lifetimes?
If it does, then what is love?
Is it merely a human experience,
Or something far greater—a spark
That connects us to the universe and to each
other,
Even long after we are gone?

Vernajh Pinder

Stitch by stitch,
I tried to create art.
I weaved your lies together,
in hopes they would become true.

Whispers of A Prism Heart

I've read tales of love stories with happy endings,
Where love was a simple happenstance or a
meet-cute,
Where amid life's ordinary pleasures,
Love fell like stardust into your lap.

I've been taught that if you believe in love,
Its symphony comes to you,
And the feeling is like an ethereal moment,
Imprinted into your bloodstream forever.

I've come to learn that until you love yourself,
Love will continue to elude you.
And not to be deceived by the moments when
you love someone,
Because ultimately, they might not love you back.

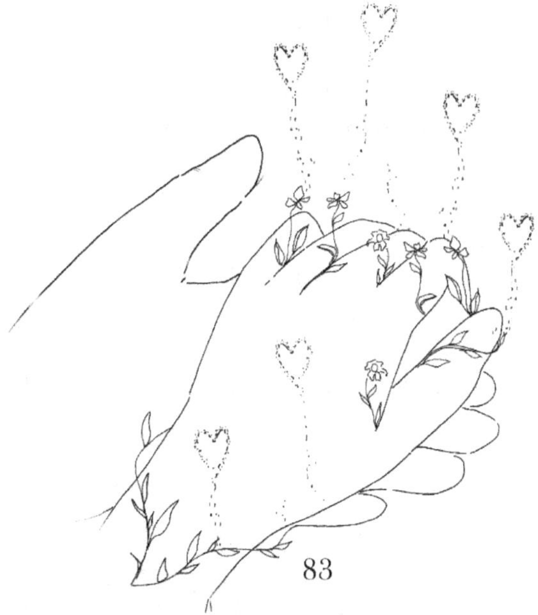

Vernajh Pinder

I could tell you how much you hurt me,
But I know you'll never truly listen.
You stood there so many times,
Watching as my eyes glistened—
Holding back tears that would soon fall.
I broke down, thinking I was losing pieces of
myself,
And you just watched.

You hurt me in ways you'll never understand.
Sometimes, I feel so broken I wonder if I can
ever be whole again.
I feel like I'm beyond repair.
You made me believe I couldn't be fixed.

Everyone tells me I'm strong enough to walk
away,
Strong enough to love myself.
But most days, I don't believe them.
Some days, I don't even want to get out of bed—
I just want to stay there, drowning in the weight
Of what I gave and lost.

I loved you with every part of me,
With every breath and ounce of life I had.
I poured it all into you.
But it was never enough.
It wasn't enough to make you happy,
To make you stay,
Or to make you choose me.

84

I was always the hardest choice.
The hardest choice, but never the right answer.

But you always got the question wrong, didn't
you?

Vernajh Pinder

I've finally allowed myself to grieve you—
To let my heart sit with the love we borrowed,
A love we had to return
Before we could truly experience it.

I've sat with the insecurities
That clung to me like shackles,
Convincing me you loved me.
But now, I let my heart speak its language,
And it whispers, over and over:
Let you go.

I've woken from my eternal slumber,
My eyes wide open at last.
I see through the lies you wrapped me in,
The false comfort of your careless caresses.

You squeezed my broken heart,
But what goes up must come down.
I've come down from the high you gave me,
The one that hypnotized me with your lies.

Now, my grief sets sail—
Leaving the harbor,
I stand on the dock,
Watching my love for you float away,
As I bathe in the embers of the moon.

I held out hope for you,
Dreaming you'd find the strength
To fight for me to stay,
To hold on just a little longer.
But you didn't,
And I can't keep waiting—
Not anymore.

Maybe it's wishful thinking,
But maybe someday,
Somehow, we'll find each other again.
In another time, another place,
We could be together.
But for now,
I have to let go.

So, my friend, this is goodbye.
Or maybe it's see you later.
Now my heart can find its peace,
Freed from the beat of yours.
But I'll always carry you with me.
I just couldn't wait forever,
And so, I had to walk away.

Whispers of A Prism Heart

Usually, I would say home is where you are,
But you are my home.
It's not wherever you are; it's where you are.
And I know that doesn't make sense, but it does.

Home is the way the multitude of stars light the
night sky,
The way warm orange, yellow, and purple hues
kiss at sunset
When the sun goes to find its first love, the
moon.
It's hard to survive without you.
In your absence, the world morphs into nothing.
And I wouldn't want to know what life was like
without you.

But with you holding my hand,
Every place feels like home.
You are my home.

Vernajh Pinder

In depths so deep,
My emotion hides—
A dance of hope,
Basking in the glow
Of Pluto's light.

Thoughts so fragile,
With ease, they disappear,
Further into the night,
Sacred mysteries
Blooming with fright.

Beneath the heart's surface,
Lies fear and fire.
It succumbs,
Layers unravel,
Of eclipsed desire.

Woven in the soul,
The story untold.
The labyrinth lays whole,
Searching for a love
To have and to hold.

Whispers of A Prism Heart

I could tell you how much I love you,
But it wouldn't even begin to make sense.
And you'll never tell me that you love me,
Because you'll always be on the fence.

Am I not worthy of it?
A little tender love and care?
Or is it because I love so hard—
Is that what has you scared?

And honestly, it breaks my heart,
Because from the jump, it's been you.
You take pieces of me every time,
And I don't know what to do.

And if I had the chance
To do it again, I would.
And as I write this piece to you,
Please don't let me be misunderstood.

Because yes, I'll always love you,
But my love's never been enough.
No, I could give you the literal universe,
And it still wouldn't be enough.

So, it's time to count my losses,
It's time for pain to cease.
It's about time I let you go,
And I pray I find some peace.

So I'll say it one more time—

Vernajh Pinder

I'd do it again, I would,
Because I hate to have to ask again:
Please don't let me be misunderstood.

Whispers of A Prism Heart

I met you in one of the darkest times of my life,
Where my sun imploded on itself and my moon
barely had life left.
I was confused about who I would be,
And if love would ever come.
The sad effects of queer youth—
Always wondering whether we would be good
enough to be loved,
To be cared for, to be seen.

Yet, you saw me, and you wanted to love me.
We exchanged numbers, and the thing I once
thought was furthest away
Became so close.
You made me feel as though love could exist,
Because I never believed in love until I met you.
I never believed in fairytales,
But you were my knight in shining armor.

You taught me that if I reached inside myself, it'd
be there.
That if I bathed in the silver glow of the moon,
The world would quiet—and it did.
The love inside my young heart bloomed like
wildflowers in a meadow.
Your touch, the alchemy that transformed my
world from "what-ifs" to "when."
Each memory, a brushstroke on this beautiful
canvas of my life.
Our love, a symphony forged in fire,

With notes never to be forgotten—a rebellion
against the world.
So, as I lay here in the meadows where I first
found you,
I gaze up at the open sky,
Where the constellations remind me of the
endless possibilities for us—
Where our love could exist and stretch infinitely
in this enchanted garden.
You taught me the magic of love,
And for that, I will always love you.

And when our time here runs out, I will still love
you—
In every lifetime, in every galaxy, in every
universe.

Our eyes locked,
And in that moment,
Our hearts collided
With each other.

"Hi," you said.
My soul leapt,
And I could see forever
In those beautiful brown eyes.

Vernajh Pinder

The raindrops dance
On the windowpane,
Our bodies tangled in the sheets.
The smell of coffee and rain fills the air,
And I hear the bustling
In the street.

Your tongue whispers my name
As I try to roll out of bed.
You pull me back in,
Kiss my forehead,
And say,
"Let's go back to sleep."

"I need to finish breakfast,"
I say.
You groan and reply,
"Breakfast is me."
I chuckle softly
And roll out of bed.

Five minutes later,
I'm scrambling eggs,
You, in your robe,
Wrap your arms around me.
I inhale your breath
As we sway, side to side.
You tell Google to play jazz,
And spin me around.
We laugh, and you look into my eyes,
Smiling as you say,

Whispers of A Prism Heart

"I've got the greatest prize."
I hold your face in my hands,
Press a kiss to your cheek,
And say, "Breakfast is ready."
You grin, hoist me onto the counter,
Kiss me softly, and murmur,
"Now we can go back to sleep."

I whisper, "Okay," against your lips,
Wrap my arms around your neck,
And we retreat to the bedroom.
You kick the door closed behind us,
And we tumble back into bed,
Giggling as we slip beneath the sheets.

Then the reality sets in—
My alarm clock is screaming at me.
I hit stop, groaning into my pillow.
It was just getting to the good part,
I think to myself,
Wishing I could dream a little longer.

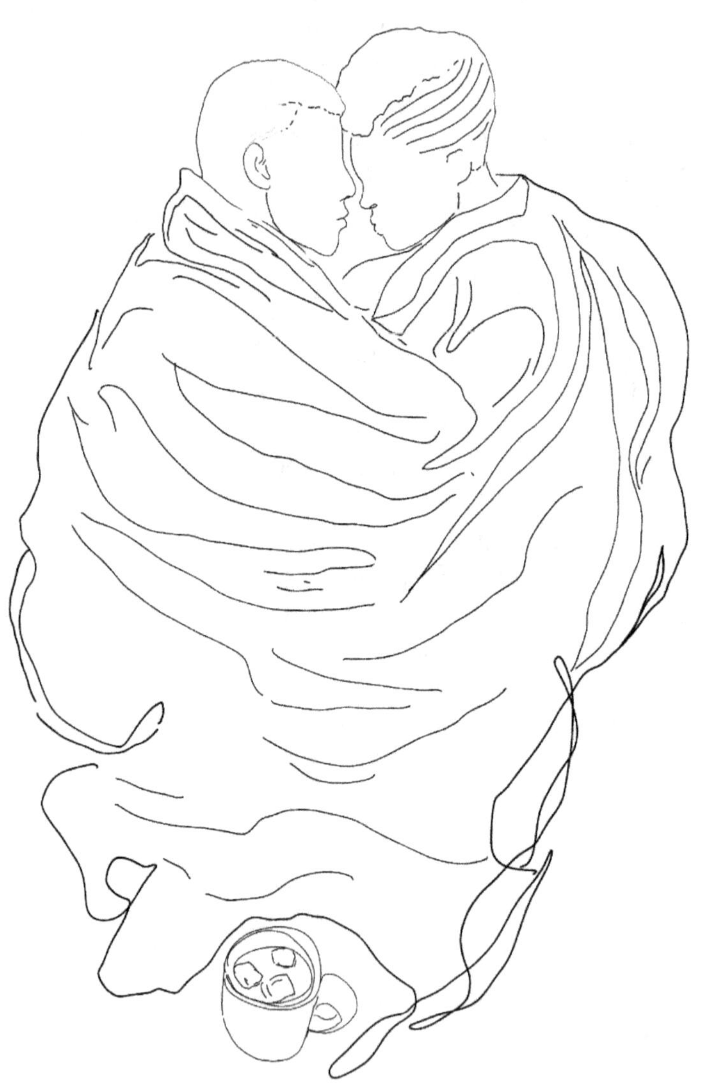

Whispers of A Prism Heart

The streets are littered
With emptiness and sorrow—
A mere reflection of my life,
And what it's been reduced to.

My existence aches for happiness,
Yet anxiety and depression
Whisper that I'm unworthy.
Love, happiness, peace—
I'm told I don't deserve them.

So, I wander these empty streets,
My dreams deferred,
Spilled onto the concrete—
A mosaic of lost potential.

There is no one out there for me.
And yet, strangely,
This solitude brings me peace.

Vernajh Pinder

I see remnants of you in the vespers of light
Pouring in through the curtains.
I hear your voice in the crackles of cigarette
ashes
Being put out in an ashtray.

I feel you in the beat of the rain,
Dancing on the tree leaves,
In the twirl of the flowers,
Swaying side to side without a care in the world.

I look around me, and you're always there,
In a simple but nuanced way.
The subtlety of your complexities remind me
That we are just specks of matter—

Little atoms existing in the density of the
universe,
Trying to find our way.
Trapped in the ghastly moments of sonder,
Our minds unraveling in the space-time
continuum.

Breaking free of a paradigm,
Nocturnal habits lie awake.
And I wear your love like my favorite hoodie,
Old, worn, threads constantly unraveling.

But woven together in black and white,
Like the temporary memories of us.

Whispers of A Prism Heart

I look at old photos of us and
 Think of old conversations,
 Letting the memories replay.
 I was once so low
 That I decided I wouldn't do this anymore.
 I thought my life began and ended with you—
 I was so love-struck, for a fool,
 A fool who'd never see the worth in me.

Vernajh Pinder

I truly thought I found love in you.
For the first time in a long time,
I felt seen—truly seen.
The walls I had spent years building,
I felt like I could let them down with you.
And so I did.

And we were fine at first.
Then something changed,
Like a switch turned off,
And you became cold and distant.
After that, I've never felt more alone
Than when I was with you.

Quick hookups, meaningless conversation—
A complete 180 from what
I had grown accustomed to.
But you were never mine to begin with.
You were on loan from someone else,
And I didn't find out until it was too late.
Until my heart beat at the same rhythm as yours,
Until my eyes could only see you.
And I stayed,
Because I don't think I've ever felt as seen
As when we first started talking.

You made me feel special, like you had won a
prize.
I felt like I had finally found my queer fairytale,
That I had found the one I would spend my life
with.

102

Clearly, I was disillusioned.
But it was fun at the time.
It felt real. It felt unconditional—
Although none of it was real.
It was a dream, and I couldn't stop myself from
free-falling,
Until I brought the whole world down with me.

I came to realize,
I never needed you—
I just needed closure.
But I also
Didn't need you
To get the closure.
It came,
Once I understood
That even if I
Sang lullabies
To the stars that night,
It would still never work out
With you.

Whispers of A Prism Heart

I dream of being so
  Drunk in love,
  That every day I wake up hungover,
  And your love is what cures that feeling.

Vernajh Pinder

Loving you was terrifying—
Not because it was hard to love you.
Quite the opposite.
You made loving you easy.

It was terrifying because it meant
Facing a version of myself
I wasn't ready to meet,
A life I wasn't ready to see—
Or couldn't see at all.

So while I was ready to love you,
I wasn't ready to love
Who I was at the time.
My unwillingness to try with you
Is a regret I carry still.

And though you've likely moved on,
Happy without me,
I find myself dreaming of us—
Holding your hand in public,
Walking down the street together,
Traveling the world side by side.

Maybe, if I had been braver,
I could have embraced the feeling
Of being truly loved.

Vernajh Pinder

Love, where did you go?
Was it my insolence
That made you cower in fear,
Only to never return?

Whispers of A Prism Heart

I often wonder what love would feel like.
Would it embrace me like purple and orange
hues embrace the evening sky?
Would it kiss me endlessly, like the moon kisses
the night?
Would it fill my lungs, letting me breathe like
oxygen does?

I've seen so many people around me
Claim to be in love—or clutch tightly to the idea
of it.
But their assumptions often breed the very
struggles
That make love feel so elusive.

To love and be loved—what an invigorating
feeling.
A feeling I hope, one day, I'll truly know.

Love, as a queer Black man,
A part of myself I've been taught to bury—
To hate, to silence, to erase.

But if I were to erase it,
I would cease to exist.
I cannot offer just fragments of myself.
We can't have pieces of me
When I am whole.

You cannot pick and choose
Which pieces of me you'll grow old with.

Vernajh Pinder

The spaceship fell.
Gravity couldn't help.
It was out of orbit,
And nothing could stop it.

Nothing stops you
When you've fallen in love.

Whispers of A Prism Heart

I've read about a love like ours,
But only in storybooks—
Carefully confined to the pages,
Like a prisoner in isolation.

And if you dare to call me by your name,
The whole world reminds us that,
Although we've made progress,
We still have a long way to go.

Vernajh Pinder

I was willing
to clip my wings,
to fall, to fade, to die—
just to ensure
you could soar
and touch the sky

Whispers of A Prism Heart

I spend most nights gazing at the stars—
they remind me of you.
Barefoot on the grass,
I let the moon sing its symphony,
a melody only I can hear.

Do you hear it?
It calls me to you,
drawing me closer to the beauty
of your galaxy—
its essence, so captivating,
so infinite,
nothing could ever prepare me
for its brilliance.

Vernajh Pinder

I never knew how much I wanted a home,
To find a place where it felt like I belong.
I'm still finding the words, still trying to find a
way.
And if I can muster up the courage
To say the words out loud,
Then my home is with you.

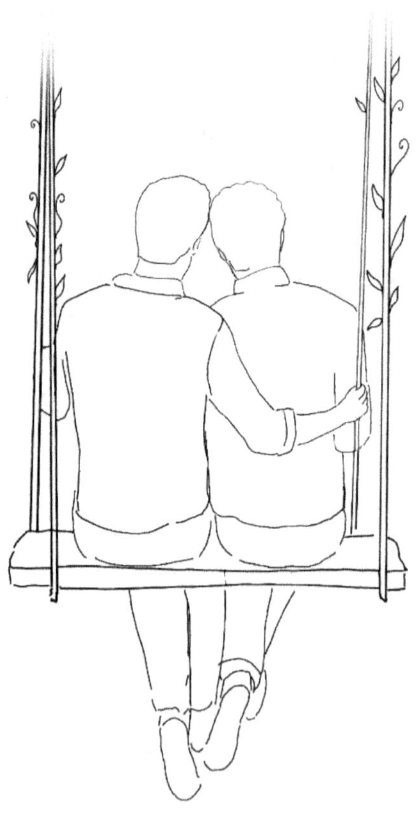

Whispers of A Prism Heart

I've dreamed of a life with you—
White picket fences and lots of greenery,
Nosy neighbors who we host
Dinner parties for,
That eventually become friends.
Kids dashing in and out of the house,
And eventually, they'll go off to college,
Make new friends, and forget about us.

But as long as I have you by my side,
I know we can get through everything—
Together.

"This is not the life you pictured but here you are. You can still make something beautiful. Grieve. Breathe. Begin again." - Thema Bryant-Davis_

CHAPTER 3
LOSS

I don't want to let go of people,
Because I know what it feels like to be let go of.
I know what it feels like to be left behind,
Like trash—forgotten, as though you were never a
part of their lives.

Discarded, like broken glass.
I know how much that hurts,
And that's why it's hard for me to let go of
people.

Vernajh Pinder

Time slips like sand through these heavy hands.
Moments once technicolor now fade to gray,
Edges softened, voices hushed.
How cruelly transitory each second feels.

I search the corners of my mind,
Chasing memories of the past.
Each one, my fickle companion,
Playing tricks with shadows—
A blurred mosaic of its former self.

Each tick of the clock becomes a haunting song,
A reminder of what I've lost.
Days that vanished like smoke in the wind,
Leaving me to mourn what's remaining.

Time, a silent thief that takes and takes,
Comes to steal youth, love, and dreams not yet
dreamt.
Its passage carves deep lines,
Endings I never thought I'd see.

Yet even in the endless trudge,
There lies a beauty—
The gift of brief moments,
Carved into the fragile walls of the heart.

And though time escapes us,
its essence lingers in what we've lived.
The paradox of loss and legacy,
its passage bittersweet,

122

an absence measured by how deeply we care.
And so, I watch the sun retreat,
its descent marking the end of another day.
Bile rises within me—
a fervent reminder to hold each passing moment
close,
before it fades into the wreckage of what's gone.

Softening cries persist,
Farewells lost in quiet departures.
Imperfect, we collide.

Vernajh Pinder

I reflect and see shadows of myself,
A child who once dreamed without prudence.
Now, these dreams lie barren,
Like a clipped bird with broken wings—
Their voices caged.

My reflection shows a person I barely know,
Etched with forehead lines from lessons learned
too late.
I search my eyes for the flames they once held,
But find only fountains of doubt—
And I stand idly by, a silent witness to all I've
lost.

The laughter that once echoed from my chest
Has become faint traces of yesterday,
A song long since swallowed by time.
Its melody drifts into an emptiness that stretches
on,
The lyrics still waiting.

Growing feels like digging a grave—
Burying parts of me to make room for more.
Each layer excavated feels heavy with grief,
A bittersweet exchange of innocence
For sapience I'm not sure I wanted.

And yet, in this grimness,
There's a silent hum of hope,
A reminder that even this pit
Holds the seeds of something new.

Perhaps, in the emptiness,
A different version of me can rise from the ashes.

Vernajh Pinder

I know you're up there,
Having a good time,
With Grammy, Aunty, Uncle,
And that cousin of mine.

I know you're at peace,
Sitting with them,
Catching them up
On all they've been missing—

About grandkids, graduations,
And everyday life,
The highs, the lows,
And everything in between.

I know you're laughing and smiling,
Drinking your favorite beer,
Dancing and singing,
Without a care in the world.

I should be happy for you,
Because you've found joy up there,
But my heart aches for you,
And it's lonely down here.

So, when you get a chance,
Could you pick up the phone?
I just want to hear your voice,
And not feel so alone.

Whispers of A Prism Heart

At 13, it hurt to breathe sometimes.
The pain was so overwhelming
That I tried to stop breathing altogether.

I grabbed a pen and wrote a note,
Laced with hate, resentment, hurt, pain, and
sadness.

I rummaged through the cupboard,
Found an unopened bottle of pills,
Went to the faucet, turned it on,
And swallowed them down, tears blurring my
vision.

I cupped my hands, washed them down,
And went back to lie down.

I cried—
And cried,
Until I lost consciousness slowly,
Until everything went black.

Hours passed,
And I regained consciousness,
But nobody found me there.
Nobody cared.

I took the note,
Ripped it up,
And never spoke of it again.
Until now...

Vernajh Pinder

I've always pondered
How different life
Would be if you didn't
Have to go back to heaven
So soon.

I was only 5 years old
When you left so suddenly,
And life has drastically changed
And morphed since then—
And I don't know.

But that's what always gets me:
The not knowing whether or not
Things would actually be different,
If things would actually change.

130

Vernajh Pinder

This world feels hollow now,
Places that once held whispers
Now reverberate with silence,
A reminder of all that's gone,
Of all that's lost.

Your absence fills the air,
A weight heavier than any presence.

I wander through these rooms,
Haunted by the ghost of your laughter.
Each step feels louder
In the emptiness you left,
As if the floor itself mourns
The sound of where your feet used to be.

The bed is vast without you,
A cavern of cold sheets and memories.
I reach for you in the dark,
But find only the edges of myself—
Pieces I once gave to you.

Love used to live here,
But now it lingers like smoke—
A trace of something burned away,
A reminder of warmth
That will never return.

Whispers of A Prism Heart

How long must I bear
The brunt of what could have been?
How long must I carry with me
This heartbreak and
These infinite memories of you?

How long must I drown myself
In the sorrow of us and what was?
How long must I mourn you
Before I can love again?
Because losing you was so unexpected.

Life is full of twists and turns,
But losing you still doesn't feel real.
Putting flowers on your grave doesn't feel real.
My hand no longer in yours,
Doesn't feel real.

I'd trade everything,
In the blink of an eye,
If it meant I could have
One last moment with you—
One last hug,
One last touch,
One last kiss.

I just want more time with you.

It's crazy how much we take time for granted,
Thinking people and places
Will always be around—

Vernajh Pinder

But nothing's promised.

Losing you taught me
To value and cherish every moment,
Because sometimes grief
Shows up unexpectedly.

It taught me to live every day
Like it's the last,
To never take it—
Not a second for granted.

Losing you taught me that life
Is but a Polaroid of mere moments,
And at any moment,
One of them could be lost forever.

So tell me—are you gone forever?
Or will I see you again in another life?

Whispers of A Prism Heart

I wish I could take your place sometimes,
Because, Lord knows, you deserve to still be
alive—
An angel sent down from heaven,
And the world wasn't ready.
It could never be ready
To lose someone as special as you.

This loss feels like the moment
Your heart stops, oxygen no longer flowing to
your brain—
Slowly, slowly, you lose yourself,
Until there's no coming back.
It feels like irreconcilable pain,
Forever lodged in my chest.

No matter how many doctors,
No matter how many surgeries,
No matter how many times they poke and prod—
It never goes away.
But eventually, it gets easier to bear,
Because you become so used to the pain,
You stop realizing it's there.
You learn to live with it—
To exist when existence feels like
A simple illusion.

Because honestly, this can't be real.
There's no way this is reality,
 And now, I have questions—
 Why would you do this?

Vernajh Pinder

Why would you take them away?
Why leave me with scars
That may never heal?
Why allow me to feel this unbearable pain?
Do you love me?
If you love me, why?
Why? Why? Why?
Why take someone who meant so much to me?
Why? Why? Why?
Why rip my heart out of my chest,
But still keep me breathing?

Whispers of A Prism Heart

I look around and see
The devastation left by your absence—
A wreckage of broken hearts,
Shattered in your wake.

Crying eyes, hollowed of their soul,
Streams of sorrow mimicking silence.
The world tilts into dysfunction,
An unbalanced realm of grief.

An overwhelming weight
Descends like twilight,
When angels return to heaven.

Yesterday, I found myself looking at old photos
of you.
I still find myself struggling with your absence.
My heart is overwhelmed with grief,
And every time I think I'll be okay,
It comes rushing back in.

I try to believe that it'll be okay,
But right now, it feels like my heart is suffering
From a thousand deaths.
It feels like my head is being held underwater,
And every time I take my last breath,
I'm brought back to life, only to repeat the cycle
again.

It feels like the entire world is imploding,
And I'm now just a passenger in my own life.
Like a fragile, weary soul,
And any form of touch will break me.

I am a wayfaring stranger,
And now that you're gone,
Nowhere feels like home.

Vernajh Pinder

In the end,
I hope you knew
How much you meant to us,
How much you lit our lives up,
And how hard it's going to be
To continue on without you.

In the end,
I hope you knew
How much talking to you
Brought a smile to our faces,
And hugging you
Made us feel safe.

In the end,
I hope you knew
How much learning from you meant,
How much we loved
Spending time with you,
Even if it was just sitting in silence.

In the end,
I hope you know
That you were loved,
In every lifetime, galaxy, and universe,
And I hope you felt loved
At the end.

Whispers of A Prism Heart

Yesterday, I turned 26, and I realized
the clock went forward,
but I've been trying to get it to go back.

I don't feel any older
than I did the day before,
and lately, you've been heavy on my mind.

It's like every little detail reminds me of you—
every smile, every laugh,
every time I see someone sip a cup of tea.

Yesterday was my first birthday without you,
and it really sucked.
I couldn't pick up the phone and call you.

I just wanted to hear your voice.
Then I realized
I'll probably never hear your voice again.

I realized that as time goes on,
I'll forget the sound of it,
and everything will fade to a distant memory.

A mere reflection,
of how things once were
but will no longer be.

I wish I could go back to a year
and a day ago,
when I had just turned 25.

141

To fly home a little more.
To call a little more.
To enjoy the little time I never knew you had
left.

They say living with the pain
of loss and grief gets easier,
that eventually, you learn to live with it.

But how could I?
How could I live with the fact
that there is an empty space where you once
stood?

Or, that you won't be here
to see me get married one day,
and that my kids
will never get to meet you?

How does my world continue to spin
when I lost the axis holding it together?

You're no longer here to see
the man that you made,
and it hurts.

It hurts because I never thought
a day would come
where I'd be left to live without you.

I thought I'd have more time to spend with you,

but when I look back,
I realize I had enough.
And that's the part that hurts the most.

Yesterday, I turned 26, and I realized
the clock went forward,
but I've been trying to get it to go back.

I don't feel any older
than I did the day before,
it's just like the clock keeps ticking by.

Vernajh Pinder

I've dreamed of all the things I could write about
you—
The story of the love you gave,
The love you shared with us,
And the ways in which you showed up.
But every time I put pen to paper,
The words in my head slip away.

Not because I can't find the words,
I could fill storybooks about you.
But writing about you like this makes it real—
To refer to you in past tense makes my heart
crumble
In on itself each time.

Knowing I'll never get to call and talk to you
again hurts.
Knowing I'll never get to hug you, laugh with
you—
That hurts.
But knowing I'll never see you again hurts like
hell,
And I don't know if I'll ever be okay.

I know you're in a better place,
And where you are, you're happy.
But the pain you left me with...
It hurts like hell.
Every day, I wake up and realize
I have to do life without you—
It makes me want to not do life at all.

144

I know you would want me to be strong,
To keep going,
But honestly, I don't know if I can.
It doesn't feel right for you not to be here.

I never liked goodbyes anyway,
So for now, I'll see you later.

He was the North Star,
Always guiding us home.
Tonight, it felt a little colder than usual,
I could see the reflection
Of my breath in the air.

I could feel his presence,
Guiding me through
The labyrinth of streets—
Left, right, straight, right, left.
It felt like he was in control.

I open the gate, jump in,
Climb into the driver's seat,
And start the engine.
Even in the quiet darkness,
I could hear his voice whispering to me.

I idle the engine,
Rocking up and down,
As the waves crash into the boat.
I take the blue flowers in my hand
And gently lay them in the ocean.

I look up and smile,
Because I know you're there,
Watching me and guiding me.
You've always been the hand I grabbed
To get me through the darkness.
And even in death,
You still watch over me.

Whispers of A Prism Heart

We grew up under the same sun,
Traded secrets under its golden glow.
Our tiny laughter echoed through endless
summers,
Your voice, a constant anchor in my world.
Now, distance has taken its place.

Your absence feels like an unfinished story,
Like chapters torn out of the book before the
ending.
Shadows of you linger in forgotten corners,
I hear your name in the breath of the wind.
Time moves, but grief stands still.

I pass places we once claimed as ours,
Backyards turned monuments of memory.
The fence still creaks,
But it holds no one now—
Just the weight of what used to be.

You were a star in my night sky,
A light I thought would never dim.
But even stars burn out,
Leaving only their glow—
And a reminder of what once was.

Vernajh Pinder

I hear the empty thud of footsteps fade,
Their resonance lost in the sands of time.
Your smile, once a song, now a cascade
Of whispers drowned by silence.

Your presence drifts, a shadow on the breeze,
Like leaves rustling, caught in autumn's sigh.
I reach, but grasp the air—
A specter in the spaces no one sees.

Your name, a pellet falling from hushed lips,
Its music swallowed by the chasm you made.
Each memory, a bullet's ricochet,
Reflecting holes of joy that slowly fade.

Though absent, still your essence leaves a stain,
A silent hum that sings of love and pain.

Whispers of A Prism Heart

Today, you were heavy on my mind.
This song came on, and it really got me thinking,
And I wondered if you truly knew—
Like, really knew—how much we loved you.

You were always there for us,
So we always knew how much you loved us.
You were at every graduation, wedding,
Awards ceremony, and special occasion,
With the biggest smile on your face.
We knew how proud you were of us,
But did you know how proud we were of you?

To have a grandfather as gentle, kind, and caring
as you—
To learn from someone as hardworking as you.
I have so many things I want to ask you,
So many things I want to say,
But I know I'll see you again one day.

So, I'll keep all my questions until then.

I built castles in my mind,
their spires reaching for skies I'd never touch.
Each stone once laid with hope,
now crumbles into dust,
leaving ruins where my heart once stood.

I hear the distant whispers of those dreams,
mocking the silence that now remains.

Yet, in mourning, there's a faint resolve—
For even in barren fields,
a seed can take root
and stretch toward another sky.

Whispers of A Prism Heart

In my haste to love you, I never stopped to love
myself.
I watched daily as I became a shadow of my
former self,
Idly watching as the smile I once loved faded,
Like the ghost of yesterday.

I was trying to get you to love me.
I was giving you all of me, and not even that was
enough.
I was willing to become lost if it meant stealing
just a minute with you.

It's funny how you once meant the world to me.
Now you're just an atom in this vast world I
share.
I've learned that I needed to trust myself,
To listen to my intuition.

I learned that even if I loved you,
I needed to love myself just a little more,
Needed to hold myself a little tighter—
Because I was always what I needed.

They say the best way to get over someone is to
get under someone else,
And for a long time, I believed that.
But really, the best way to get over someone
Is to fall in love with yourself first,
To put who you are—your thoughts, your
feelings, your being—

Above everyone else.

So, as much as I wanted someone to love me,
I had to learn to love myself first.

I never liked goodbyes anyway,
But I think this is goodbye, after all.

Whispers of A Prism Heart

You hold me as if the world might break,
As if time itself could shatter at any moment.
Each breath is a fragile promise,
A thread connecting us to the unknown.

Your absence looms,
A dark hole pulling at the edges of my mind.
I feel the silence you left behind—
The echo of your laughter,
A ghost haunting spaces we once shared.

And yet, I love you fiercely,
Even as this darkness continues to grow.
Because what is love, if not the courage
To hold onto something,
Knowing that at any moment, it could slip away?

Vernajh Pinder

The streets fell silent, heavy with despair,
A sentiment that stretched across nations.
The world mourned together,
A loss etched into time.
The world felt smaller.

Our faces, trapped behind masks, were mirrors,
Reflecting grief too painful for words.
The air carried whispers of lives unlived,
Charred remains of dreams now on hold,
And a stench that seeped into every corner.

Yet, in the chaos, we found fragments of love—
Hands reaching through screens,
Hearts beating in unison.
In our shared pain, we endured—
Brittle, but fiercely alive.

It's okay to grieve what you've lost—
Whether that's a friendship, a relationship, or
even a family member.
Grieving is a part of life, and sometimes we hold
on to things that aren't really there,
Hoping, wishing, that things will change.
Allow yourself the space to grieve what's lost.
Feel those emotions fully,
And only then will you be able to move on.

Vernajh Pinder

Hushed whispers, never speaking my name,
Love, a shadow cast upon the wall,
A house of blood, all the same,
A hollow silhouette of his former self.

Love should never be bartered, bought, or sold,
Nor clipped like wings.

At night, my heart unravels, fiber by fiber,
An absence lingering heavy on my chest.
Yet still, I rise—
Carving a home where love is the framework.

Though their hands have left my shoulders bare,
My soul still sings.

Whispers of A Prism Heart

If things were difference and you could stay
awhile,
Would your laughter fill the spaces we once
knew?
Would your love still linger,
And paint the sky in pink and orange hues?

Would I walk a path both safe and bright,
Untarnished by the force of all I've lost?
Would dreams take flight, unworn by grief?
or would my light be the cost?

Perhaps my heart would never ache
Or long for ghosts that never came.
Perhaps my heart would never bend or break,
A foreigner to the touch of pain.

Yet even here, in worlds you remain,
I wonder—would I still have grown the same?

Eventually, it gets easier. The urge to text them, the urge to call them and hear their voice, the urge to see them, touch them, be near them—eventually, all those urges fade away, and you find yourself fine. You don't miss them, you don't think about them, you don't feel like you need them anymore. But to get there...Well, that takes time.

I wanted to mend people. To hold, in my hand, the tenuous pieces of their stories and tell them they were whole, even when the world tried to teach them otherwise. I took note of the way pain would settle into the corners of a their's eyes, how their silence would scream louder than their words, and how a single breath could carry years of weight. Psychology was my calling (or so I thought).

But dreams, I learned, are not always tended; sometimes, they are ripped from the soil before they ever have the chance to take root. No one will talk to a Black psychologist, she said, her voice a blatant disregard against my gentle ambitions. I carried her words with me like my favorite stuffed animal. Was she right? Maybe the world would look at my skin before they saw me and my knowledge.

So, I let it go. I packed away dream in moving boxes and left them to gather dust. But even now, I wonder—who would I have became if I never taped those boxes shut? Would I have sat across from someone who needed me, held space for them? Would I have assured them that healing was possible? Or would I have spent my days proving my worth to a world unwilling to listen, unwilling to see me?

Letting go changes you. It leaves a empty space where dream once lived, so full of life. But I have learned that even when dreams go to die, the hunger to keep dreaming never does. Maybe I won't be a psychologist, but I can still be a healer. I can still continue to weave words together on pages, allowing them the space and freedom to touch the hearts of those who dare to read them. Maybe things won't turn out the way I imagined, but in the way it was always meant to be.

"For me, becoming isn't about arriving somewhere or achieving a certain aim. I see it instead as forward motion, a means of evolving, a way to reach continuously toward a better self. The journey doesn't end." — Michelle Obama

CHAPTER 4
BECOMING

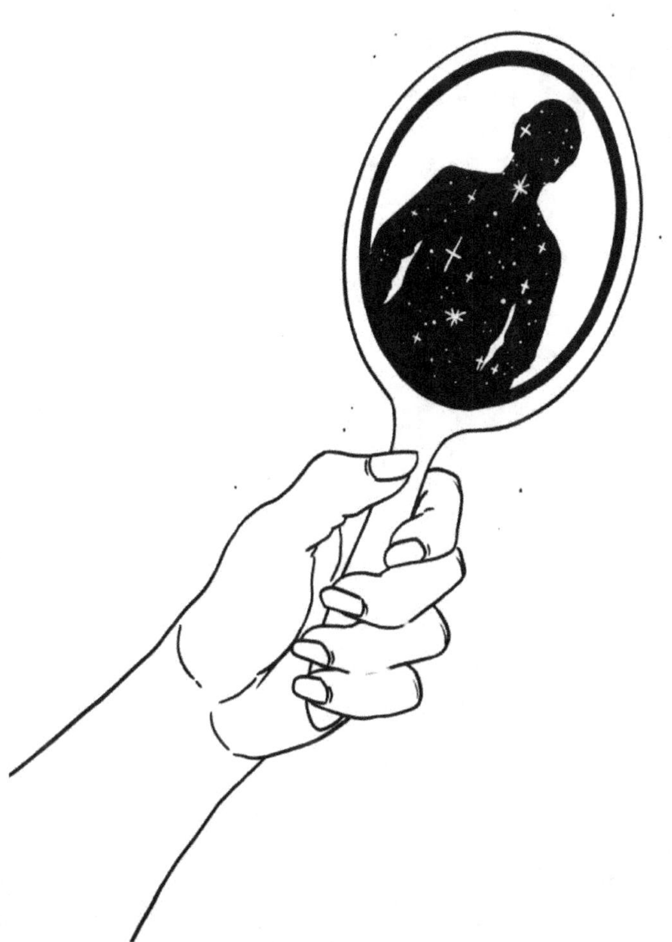

Whispers of A Prism Heart

Wherever you go,
 Wherever this world may take you,
 Life will try to break you down.

But remember:
You are more than your wildest dreams.

Life may make you feel small,
Like you must shrink to fit its mold.

Never shrink.
Always stand tall.

Be proud of who you are,
For you are light,
And the world needs you to shine.

Journal Entry 2: Life Mysteries - June 17, 2023 - 3:05 PM

I write this from the couch in my living room on a warm summer day. The air inside is cold, I've just eaten half of an edible, and I'm listening to 25 in Barcelona. Ironically, for the past year, I've been saying I'd turn 25 in Barcelona, but that's still up for debate. It's so crazy how little things can influence such big parts of your life. People, places, songs, and things—all of these shape the person you become. Strange, isn't it? When we sit down and pause for a moment, we realize how much of what we think is important isn't really that significant. But living life, that's what matters. We get so obsessed with reaching our goals, our futures, our dreams, that we spend so much of our time running. Running toward them, pushing the goalposts back further and further. Until we're 70, sitting outside on the patio, watching an evening sunset in Barcelona, and we wonder why it took us so long to enjoy life's beauty. Why did we allow ourselves to miss out on so much? Our obsession with the future made us forget to live in the now. To be present. To embrace the moments we have now because, in reality, it's all we have.

A wise writer once wrote that we should live in the now because the past is gone, and the future isn't promised. I sit here pondering this because it's absolutely true. Though we reminisce about the past because of the happiness and nostalgia it brings, and we dream about the future because it gives us hope, what do these little moments of now give us? Despair? Pain? Sadness? I remember when I got my heart broken for the first time, and I thought life was going to end. Hell, I even tried to help the process. I was so engrossed in the now that no future could tell me it would get better because I wouldn't believe it. Now, look at me— in my Monica era because I'm so over you. But, a part of me never thought I'd get here. To be happy in life without someone who played a significant role in it. To think I'd be growing up without friends I once grew up alongside. Family members who took care of me. It's hard to imagine I'd be here. Chasing the dreams I talked about with them. I'm here, but they're not. I was so engrossed in the future that I forgot to live in the present with them, and now all that's left are fading memories I'm no longer sure if I conjured up or if that's what actually happened. Because memories aren't as accurate as we think.

So here we have three different concepts: the past, the present, and the future. Three things so intertwined that without one, the other two wouldn't exist. The past leads to our present and helps us become who we need to be for the future. The future gives us hope in the present, regardless of our past. The present lets us see how far we've come and how far we still have to go. And in either's absence, we are merely devoid. Energies of nothingness floating through a galaxy. Particles of stardust, only existing because we have the stars. Little iotas. Floating sound waves searching for the right frequency. The vast deuterium of human existence. Challenged. Questioned. Put to the forefront.

I am the past, present, and future. My existence, merely a bane in the mysteries of life.

Whispers of A Prism Heart

I read a poem once,
It said,
"Three things are certain:
We are born,
We die,
We grow."

I don't agree.
Only one thing is certain in this life—
We die.

Not everyone gets a chance
To be born or to grow.
Some of us are lucky,
Others, not so much.

Which is why,
For those of us
Who are born
And get to grow,
We must live.

We must utilize
Every ounce of life
That we have,
Because we never know
When it's our time to say goodbye.

Today, you turn twenty-six—a milestone not all young Black men get to celebrate. For 26 years, you've been a blessing to so many, both known and unknown. You've helped others create, dream, and simply exist. Your light—a quiet, powerful aura—gives those around you permission to be themselves.

I pray that your twenties continue to be kind to you. May you savor every moment and make the most of this beautiful life. You've endured so much and emerged resilient, inspiring others with your strength. You are the hope and dreams of Black boys who look like you, feel like you, and are you. You give them a reason to carry on and fight.

When you feel like you're losing ground or hope, remember this: You are enough. You are valued, cherished, and deeply loved. You are worthy of happiness and peace. Keep setting the tone for others—your dedication and creativity are unmatched, and the legacy you're building will be unforgettable.

I know we often encourage you to open up about your feelings. We do this not to pry, but because we care deeply about your happiness. To become the best version of yourself, you must allow yourself to heal.

Healing isn't a destination; it's a journey—a choice you make every day, even when it hurts. The experiences that have shaped you have made you strong enough to reach this point, but to grow further, you must let go of the pain. You deserve to heal. You are healing.

Know this: You don't have to carry every burden alone. It's okay to ask for help. When you can't carry it all, I'll be here to share the load. I'll love you even when you struggle to love yourself—and in those moments when you do.

Take time to reflect on how far you've come. You've dedicated yourself to every endeavor and infused your creativity into everything you touch. You remind me of a butterfly—fragile yet strong, drawn to the light and embodying transformation.

I hope you take the time to explore the world, seize every moment, and embrace the beauty around you, within you, that is you.

You are beautiful and powerful beyond measure. Thank you for allowing me to be part of your journey. And if you remember nothing else, know this: In every lifetime, every universe, every reality, you are loved by me.

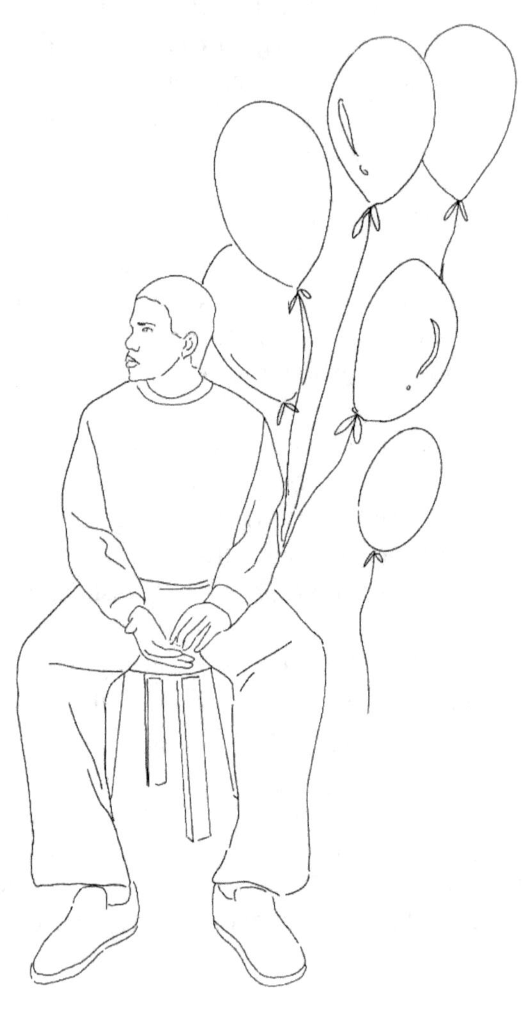

Whispers of A Prism Heart

My pen has searched for depth,
While my mind has searched for purpose.
Neither apologizing to the other,
For leaving the other behind.

Vernajh Pinder

I often wonder what it means to be whole,
To exist without the pieces I've given away,
Each fragment left behind with someone who left
me.

But now, in the silence of my own creation,
I begin to reclaim myself,
Gathering the scattered parts,
And stitching them together, piece by piece.

It's not the same as it once was,
But it is mine.
This is me—whole and imperfect,
And finally, at peace.

W

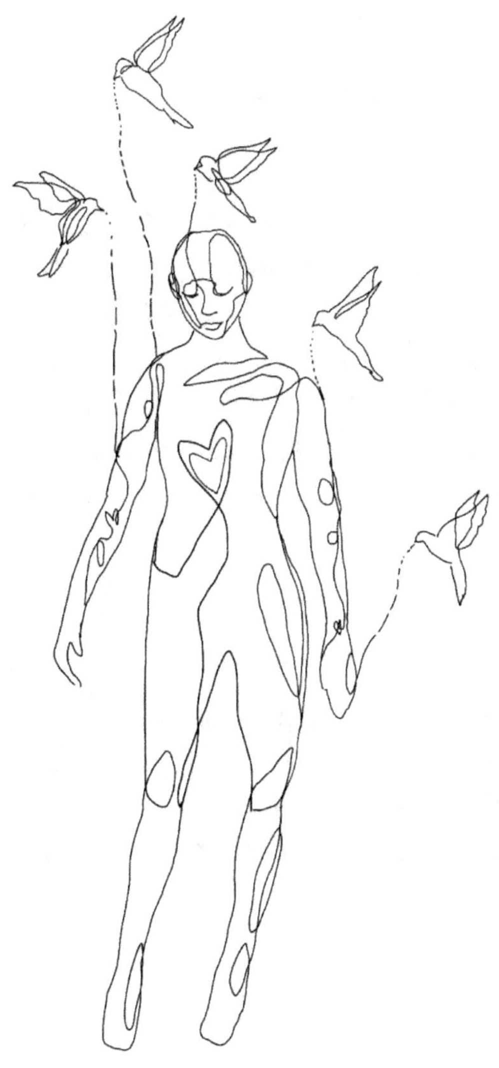

Journal Entry 3

I've been questioning myself a lot lately. Why am I the way I am? Why do I let myself get so easily provoked to anger? Why do I give people that power over my peace? What am I really scared of? Do their words actually hurt, or is it just that I'm full of hurt myself? Is this my way of standing up for myself now, in a way I couldn't when I was younger? Why am I so angry? Does it hurt because there's some truth to what they're saying, or is it just the audacity of it all?

I don't want to be an angry person anymore. I just want peace. I just want love. I don't want to feel like my world is spinning off its axis, and that I'm losing control. So, I breathe, and I count to 10. I smile, lift my head, and walk away because, really, is it worth it? Does anyone truly deserve that much power, that much control over me?

We are all extraordinary individuals with innate talents and abilities. We journey through life searching for our purpose, trying to find a reason to be alive, a reason for why we go through these events in our lives, and a reason for our existence. We want to change the lives of the people we encounter, for them to say, "Because I met you, I knew I could do better, I tried a little harder, or I loved a little deeper."

So, how do you want to be remembered? Do you want to be remembered for your kind heart, for your grit and resilience, for your optimism, and for your words?

May your words continue to live on in the hearts and minds of those who dare to dream, who dare to fight, and who dare to be alive. May your words inspire generations and instill in them hope for the future, a passion to keep trying, and the will to live and fight another day.

Vernajh Pinder

I thought coming out to my parents
Would be the hardest thing I'd ever do.
I thought they'd hate me,
Disown me,
But they welcomed me with an overwhelming
amount of love.
(Not a lot of queer kids can say that.)

Yet, I wished they had shunned me,
Ridiculed me,
Because then it would make sense—
The names they called me,
The venom they spat from their lips,
And I'd have to drink the poison every time.

The way they made me feel—
I shrunk myself,
Trapped the real me in a closet,
Because I thought it was safer
Than ever telling them I was queer.

And now, I'm faced with questions
That I still don't have the answers to:
If you love me like you say you do,
Why would you hurt me the way you did?

Whispers of A Prism Heart

Showing up for yourself
Is so hard sometimes,
Hard to muster up
The courage to be you.
But sometimes, you have to
Ignore those voices in your head,
Put your best clothes on,
And show up for you.

Vernajh Pinder

The older I get,
The more I realize
My capacity for things
That no longer serve me
Has dwindled to nothing.

I'm not fighting for anything.
Not a friendship.
Not a relationship.
Not a damn thing.
I'm tired of fighting.

Especially when the things
You fight for
Don't fight back for you.
So, then what's the point
When you're all in this alone?

The reality of it is, no matter how much I try to absolve you of the pain you inflicted on me, every time I see you, I remember. This wound will probably take forever to heal, and the messed-up part is, you'll never understand how I feel. I don't even think you'll take accountability for the part you played and the lies you told.

While I want to hate you, that's the easiest part. What's harder is forgiving you for the role you played in this. What's even harder is forgiving myself for allowing it to happen. I kept thinking things would get better, that they would change, but deep in my heart, I knew they wouldn't, and I held onto a false hope I created to make my decisions feel right. I allowed myself to live a delusional life, and now I'm paying the price.

So, I forgive myself.

Evolution is a sticky process.
As we grow and shed the parts of us that no
longer serve us,
We have to come to terms with the person we
are becoming.

As we transition through these various stages of
life,
I've come to realize that the hardest person to
forgive
Is the one we see in the mirror.

The weight is heavy,
Holding onto so much pain,
Thinking it would protect us,
But it became our armor.

But in the end,
It only keeps us bound.
The more we resist change,
The faster it finds us.

Eventually, in losing who we were,
We become who we were meant to be.

Do you ever get so caught up in your head that life passes you by? Every moment, every memory, every person—in the blink of an eye, it's like the galaxy shrinks, and you're floating into oblivion, watching as everything around you speeds past. You try to reach out and grab a memory, but as soon as you touch it, it's gone, and a million more images zoom by. You watch as friendships and lovers grow apart from you. You watch as family, friends, and your kids age, and there's nothing you can do to stop it. You've taken a passenger seat in your own life, and there's nothing you can do to stop it.

Vernajh Pinder

It took a long time, but I've reconciled with the
fact
That parents are not perfect.

We all come with our baggage,
And unless we actively unpack it,
We end up hurting people.

Our parents were once us,
And some of them didn't have the tools
They needed to properly assess and process.

So, they end up in a vicious cycle
Where they hurt people.
It's endless.

Sometimes, in healing yourself,
You realize that you can't solicit love
From people who don't understand the concept.

Some people aren't able to give themselves love.
They are humans like us,
Trying to figure life out,
And just like us, they make mistakes.

Hold people accountable for the roles they play,
But forgive them so you can grow
Into the person you're meant to become.

It's hard,
But it's necessary.

I'm in a season of my life where I'm constantly growing and evolving. There comes a point where the person you are now no longer serves the person you're striving to be in the future. You become like a snake, shedding your skin. You sit in solitude and reflect—reflect on where you are and what you need to do to get to where you're going.

Vernajh Pinder

To say this year has been tumultuous would be putting it mildly. I've experienced the joys of love, happiness, and peace, while also enduring the tragedies of death, grief, and loss. I've mourned old lives and celebrated new ones. I've created happy memories with people who are no longer with me and have had to learn how to navigate life without them. I've experienced the highest of highs and the lowest of lows. I've collected memories and heartaches. I've lost myself, found myself, and lost myself again. Right now, I'm still finding myself—still figuring out who I am and who I want to be. Each day, I show up authentically as myself and give myself the space and opportunity to live: to show up, to be present, and to live in the moment. Because if this year has taught me anything, it's that all we have is right now.

To the little boy,
Who tried to end his life
In the 9th grade,

To the little boy
Who cried himself to sleep,

To the little boy
Who didn't know
Who he wanted to be,

To the little boy,
Who felt like
He wasn't good enough,

To the little boy
Who thought he'd never find love
Or that he didn't deserve it,

To the little boy
Who hated his reflection
In the mirror,

To the little boy
Who read books
To escape his reality,

To the little boy
Who was scared
To love out loud,

It gets better,
And I'm proud of you.
Hold on just a little longer,
Your wounds have made you stronger.

Chin up, one day you'll see—
Little boy, you are me.
No, it's not easy getting here,
But your scars are the beauty.

And when you feel scared,
Know that you have me.
Call my name, I'll find you,
And I'll always be there.

Because every step of the way,
When you get lost,

Look yourself in the mirror,
And know I will be there.

Whispers of A Prism Heart

In the grand scheme of things,
Life is an optical illusion—
A Polaroid picture
Of simple moments,
Slipping through your hands.

You can spend all your life
Trying to grab and capture those tiny grains,
Or you can embrace the ebb and flow.

You can exist and live,
Or remain afraid.

As I sit here and reflect on the past few days, I am overcome with gratitude. I'm grateful that the powers that be allowed everything to align and work out for me. This reminds me that I am exactly where I need to be. But I'd be remiss if I wasn't honest and said that it gives me anxiety. The future now has an unknown element, and while I'll cross that bridge when I get there, I still somehow feel stuck there. It's like driving in the fog, and you can't see what's on the other side. I guess that's why you go slow and take the necessary precautions. I try to plan in advance, but even with a plan, there are still roadblocks. The unexpected can happen in the blink of an eye, and the only thing you can do is pivot.

So, I ask myself now, what is the obsession with control? Am I hurt because my seven-year-old self had to do as he was told? That he had no control over his life, even when he turned 12 or 14? Is this to make up for that? Does the loss of control make me feel like a hurt child again? I'm unsure of the answer.

Moreover, it seems I make enemies everywhere I go. Is it my entitled behavior, like something is owed to me because we are all on loan here, and at any moment, the debt collector can come to collect his debt?

Nonetheless, I like when things go my way, but when they don't, it feels like a crater has formed in the world, and now it's sinking. An implosion waiting to happen. Why is that? Why do I feel like I'm always right? That my way is the best course of action? Is it because I never felt listened to as a kid? I felt unheard and unseen. I didn't feel loved, did I? I'm sure that's a part of it.

Is it all in my head? Have I created my own pain, my own anxiety? My thoughts race sometimes—so fast that the only way for them to stop is to grab each one and speak to it. To engage in egregious conversations so that I can be left alone. I'm reminded every day that in order to become the person I want to be, I have to do something I've never done. This time of transformation requires discipline, self-reflection, solitude, and silence. But with silence comes the voices, the taunts, the whispers, and the provocation.

Peace was not an idea I stumbled upon. It wasn't the light waiting for me at the end of some dark tunnel, nor was it handed to me wrapped in a cute little bow. No. It was a battle—vigorous, dark, and unrelenting. I fought to find it, and sometimes, I wasn't sure if it was even worth the fight.

I had to confront the parts of myself I'd long tucked away. The child who cried quietly in the corner, the teenager who hated his own reflection, the adult who wore a mask so the world couldn't see he was crumbling inside. Each version of me held a piece, and I couldn't ignore them anymore.

The journey was messy. I screamed and begged for answers from the heavens, Only to be rewarded with silence. But it was in that silence that I learned to listen—to the whispers of my heart, to the remnants of my own breath. Slowly, I realized peace wasn't a destination. It was in the minuscule moments: The softness of sunlight on my face, the wetness of my feet touching the grass, the warmth of hope that I gave myself.

I stopped running, and I sat with the weight of my failures, my fears, my flaws, and found that they didn't make me not enough—they made me real.

Peace wasn't just given to me. I built it, brick by fragile brick, within the ruins of who I used to be. Now, it lives in me as a reminder that even in chaos, I can find moments to breathe, and that, in the end, I'm always becoming.

I write stories,
Weaving words onto the page,
Etching feelings into the hearts
Of those who read.

My poetry dances like shadows,
Silhouetted beneath the moonlight.
My art is a symphony,
Kissing the lips of those
Who dare to live,
Who dare to see,
Who dare to dream,
And believe they can become.

Whispers of A Prism Heart

I laid my past upon the ground,
And let its weight press into the earth,
Leaving marks I knew would never fade.

The pain clung to me,
Like a shadow, always present.
I let it fall,
And as I began to loosen my grip,
I watched it scatter in the wind.

Vernajh Pinder

Wherever you go,
Wherever this world may take you,
Life will beat you down sometimes.
But always remember:
You are greater than your wildest dreams.

Life may make you feel like you must shrink
yourself,
But never shrink.
Always stand tall.
Always be proud of who you are.

Whispers of A Prism Heart

My mind wilts away,
And the words never come.
Where flowers once bloomed,
Ideas now go to die.

My pen limits me,
And my brain
No longer nourishes
Enough for me to grow.

The happiness that once lived inside
Has now died.

Becoming is a delicate balance, like walking a tightrope stretched between who you are and who you want to be.

The pursuit of becoming isn't about rushing to the other side. It's about the grace in each step, the strength to steady yourself after every wobble, and the courage to keep going despite the unknown.

Silence is not the absence of sound,
But the presence of something deeper—
An invitation to listen to what the world, and
your soul,
Has been trying to say all along.

At first, it was uncomfortable,
Like standing in a dark room where every
shadow felt menacing.
My thoughts were loud, my doubts deafening.
But I stayed. I sat with the quiet,
Letting it press into my soul.
Slowly, the noise inside me began to fade.

In silence, I've learned to listen to the sounds of
my own breath.
It was in doing this that I unearthed truths buried
beneath:
The pain I ignored, the questions I avoided,
The parts of myself I tried to silence—
All stood to meet me.
And instead of running away, as I usually do, I
listened.

This space became my sanctuary,
Not because it erased the pain,
But because it gave me room to hold it gently.
Silence reminds me that I am whole,
Even in the moments I feel broken.
And that within the quiet lies the power to begin
again.

Whispers of A Prism Heart

The stars whisper stories
Older than memory,
Reminding me that existence
Is both fragile and infinite.

As I gaze upward,
I am reminded of this truth:
We are all made of the same light.

Vernajh Pinder

Inner calm is but a fragile flame,
Flickering in the face of life's winds.
It glows steady, quieting the chaos.

I've learned to cherish the moments when calm
finds me.
In those instants, the world feels manageable,
My thoughts aligned, my heart steady.
But peace is not permanent;
It's a gift that demands presence,
A state that asks to be held gently, but never
gripped.

The challenge is not in chasing it,
But in accepting its impermanence.
To let it come and go,
Trusting that it will return when the storms pass.
It's in this acceptance, this surrender,
That we find the strength to endure.

Whispers of A Prism Heart

I'm sorry I wasn't adequate enough for you,
And that you thought you could treat me like all
the ones before me.
I'm sorry I didn't stay through your manipulation
and lies,
Because I knew I deserved better.

I'm sorry I loved you when I really should have
left you.
I'm sorry I gave you parts of me that I should've
kept for myself.
I'm sorry I had hope that you could change,
Because who you are now will always be your
nature.

I'm sorry for every time I said "I love you" and
meant it,
Because you are not deserving of any essence of
my love.
I'm sorry for the months I wasted on you,
The tears I cried over you,
Because I could've put them to better use.

I'm sorry I gave you the opportunity to be in my
presence,
Because I will always be too much for you—
Too much for you to love,
Too much for you to trust,
Or to be yourself around.

I'll always be too much for you.

Whispers of A Prism Heart

It all begins with hesitation.
This moment where my pride and vulnerability
collide.
I scroll past your name a thousand times,
The weight of all left unsaid feels heavy.
Our laughter now a distant memory—
Familiar, but too far away.

I wonder if you feel it too.
The absence.
This hollow space where we used to stand,
shoulder to shoulder.
I wonder if you replay the arguments or the silent
battles.
Or maybe you've moved on,
Carrying only faint pieces of what we once
shared.

But today, I chose differently.
I chose to hold space for what we had,
Instead of mourning what we lost.
I let go of the resentment,
And the need to create a villain in this story.
There is no winner in the aftermath of us—
Just two people who grew apart,
Caught in the streams of life.

No matter how much it hurts, don't stop allowing yourself to feel. When you stop feeling, you begin to numb yourself, losing touch with reality. You miss out on the great moments in your life because you allowed someone else to control your emotions. We aren't giving people that kind of power anymore.

Whispers of A Prism Heart

I sit at the edge of the world,
Where the darkness kisses the light,
And all the worries that once sat with me
dissolve,
Washed away by the tide.

The salt air wraps around me,
A comfort for the noise within.

Vernajh Pinder

The waves speak in hushed tones,
a language older than time.
Each crest, a gentle exhale;
each fall, a quiet return.
Their rhythm steadies my breath,
pulling me into their calm.
I sit at the edge of the world,
where the sea kisses the shore,
and the worries I carry dissolve,
washed away with the tide.
The salt air wraps around me,
a balm for the noise within.
Here, amidst the endless ebb and flow,
I find serenity—not in answers,
but in the constancy of the waves.
They remind me that even in motion,
there is peace to be found.

Whispers of A Prism Heart

I am learning to take the leap, even when fear
Beckons me to stand still.
Even when its hands press against my chest,
Telling me that the unknown
Is sharper than the wounds I've already worn.

For I have spent too long in the quiet,
Between who I am and who I am afraid to be.

Even if the road ahead is one I cannot see,
I will walk it anyway.
Because fear may whisper,
But I will not let it write my story.

Vernajh Pinder

I hope you understand that your feelings are
                                    valid,
And that one day, you'll give yourself the space,
                        The love, the grace to heal,
                        Because you deserve it.

                    You are allowed to feel, to exist,
                    To simply be—without warrant.
                    You don't need a reason to be you.

May you blossom like a wild sunflower,
                    Even though they try to bury you.

Whispers of A Prism Heart

I didn't understand your struggles until I grew
into my own.
I never could understand the sacrifices you
made,
Until I had to make some of my own.

If anger is a wildfire, then forgiveness is the rain.
My anger burned like a matchstick—
Quick to ignite, but fleeting with perspective.
And once that came,
Guilt whispered lies into my ears,
Hoping I would believe them.
And at one point, I did.

But as they say,
"Hindsight is 20/20."

Growth feels like breaking,
But the pieces know how to reshape themselves.
A fracture first, then slow repair with time,
Like wilted leaves that learn to kiss the sun,
Or echoes softening into silent rhyme.

You have helped me understand so much about myself. You've given me the space I needed to heal and grow. You've taught me that love comes to those who wait, and that one day, I would attract the love I deserve, not the one I settled for.

Vernajh Pinder

Growth sometimes feels like stretching too far—
like almost breaking, but not quite. We meet
countless versions of ourselves, releasing the parts
we no longer need. Yet, sometimes, we cling to
these past selves, bringing flowers to their grave
and singing hymns, hoping for one more meeting.

I've learned that while these versions were vital—
Instrumental in our journey—they must be
released. It's like climbing a mountain; The trek is
hard, but each step brings us closer to the peak.
Two truths can exist: We can look back and
admire how far we've come, but we must keep
moving forward to reach the summit. And
sometimes, that means leaving those versions
behind.

ABOUT THE
AUTHOR

Vernajh Pinder is a poet from the Bahamas with a deep passion for literature, music, art, and culture. An avid reader and storyteller, he explores themes of love, identity, and human connection through his poetry. Vernajh holds a Bachelor of Science in Hospitality and Tourism Management from the University of Maryland Eastern Shore, as well as a Master's in Counselor Education with a specialization in school counseling. His work reflects his diverse experiences and love for creative expression. Stay connected with him on Instagram: @vernthepoet.

www.ingramcontent.com/pod-product-compliance
Lightning Source LLC
Chambersburg PA
CBHW060314310726
48976CB00007B/2328